Edmund Maturin

The Origin of Christianity in Ireland: A Lecture

SALZWASSER
VERLAG

Edmund Maturin

The Origin of Christianity in Ireland: A Lecture

Reprint of the original, first published in 1859.

1st Edition 2022 | ISBN: 978-3-37512-218-8

Verlag (Publisher): Salzwasser Verlag GmbH, Zeilweg 44, 60439 Frankfurt, Deutschland
Vertretungsberechtigt (Authorized to represent): E. Roepke, Zeilweg 44, 60439 Frankfurt, Deutschland
Druck (Print): Books on Demand GmbH, In de Tarpen 42, 22848 Norderstedt, Deutschland

THE ORIGIN OF CHRISTIANITY IN IRELAND.:

A LECTURE

DELIVERED BEFORE

THE HALIFAX CATHOLIC INSTITUTE,

ON TUESDAY EVENING, NOVEMBER 1, 1859.

BY EDMUND MATURIN, A. M.,

(President.)

HALIFAX, N. S.

PRINTED FOR THE CATHOLIC INSTITUTE,

By Compton & Bowden.

1859.

THE ORIGIN OF CHRISTIANITY IN IRELAND.

On the last occasion on which I had an opportunity of delivering a
Lecture before this Association, I selected for my subject " the Origin
of Christianity in England," and it was my great design to show,
from historical evidence, that, from the period of the first commencement of the Christian Religion in that country down to the time of
the final disruption in the 16th Century, the Church of England was
always regarded as an integral part of the Catholic Church, in full
communion with the See of Rome. And now, I shall proceed to con-
tinue the same inquiry with reference to another of the British Islands,
in which I am sure that we all take the deepest interest, and with which
most of us are more or less directly connected, by birth or by descent,
as the home of our youth and the land of our fathers, which, after all
its political and religious revolutions, and after all the various vicissi-
tudes in our own lives, is so dear to memory still, and so closely associated with all the sacred recollections of past events in the national
and Ecclesiastical History of Ireland.

It may be observed, then, that there are three great events which
must be taken into consideration, in order to understand the present
religious situation of Ireland. The first is the introduction of Christianity into the country—the second is the English invasion of the
kingdom in the 12th Century—and the third is the legal establishment of the Protestant Reformation in the 16th Century. These
may be regarded as the principal elements out of which the present
condition of the country has grown, and their effects are clearly per-
ceptible in every part of Ireland to this day. I must, however, con-
fine myself chiefly to the first of these on the present occasion, as my
purpose is to speak of the *earliest period* of the history of the Irish
Church, of the principal *Missionaries* by whom the Faith of Christ

was planted in that country, and of the general nature of the *doctrines* which they delivered to the infant Church, as derived from the most authentic sources of information.

The first point of inquiry, to which our attention is directed, relates to the *time* when the Gospel was first preached in Ireland, and the *individuals* who were engaged in its propagation. But, unfortunately, we have no means of arriving at any satisfactory conclusion on these points. It must be confessed, and it is rather a discouraging confession, that the history of the introduction of Christianity into Ireland is involved in impenetrable obscurity. It is now impossible to ascertain the precise time, at which Christianity was originally introduced into the country. This is generally admitted by all Ecclesiastical historians, both Catholic and Protestant. Perhaps this may appear strange to some of you, who are accustomed to associate the memory of St. Patrick with the very existence of the Christian Faith among the ancient inhabitants of Ireland. It may be asked—Was not St. Patrick the Apostle of Ireland, and the Founder of the Irish Church? Now this is certainly true *in one sense*, but it is not true *in another sense*, and therefore it is necessary to enter into a more particular explanation on these points, in order to construct our system of Church History on a solid foundation. In the first place, then, it is certain that St. Patrick was not the first person who was sent to Ireland by the Apostolic See, nor was he originally invested with Episcopal authority for the government of the Church, and the conversion of the natives to the Faith of Christ. The individual who was appointed to this commission, though he preceded St. Patrick by a very short interval of time, was Palladius, of whom I shall soon have occasion to speak more fully, but at present I merely notice the fact, in order to present a clearer view of the order of events. But further, as the learned Dr. Lanigan remarks, " it is universally admitted, that there were Christian congregations in Ireland, before the mission of Palladius, which took place in 431."* How, or when, or by whom, these Christian congregations were formed, we have no direct evidence in the records of antiquity, and we are therefore left very much to probable conjectures, founded upon indirect allusions or remote anal-

---

* Lanigan's Ecclesiastical History, Vol. I. p. 9. (Ed. Dub. 1822.)

ogies. In my former Lecture, I referred to the great want of historical information which can be derived from the writings of the ancient Fathers on the earliest Church History of England, and I regret to say, that we have to complain of the same want still more strongly with reference to Ireland, as I am not aware of a single passage from any of the Christian Fathers which can be brought forward in illustration of the subject. Poor Ireland, from its remote situation and insular position, seems to have been so entirely cut off from all Ecclesiastical communication with the rest of the world, in those days, that it appears to have almost escaped the notice of the great writers of the Church, or at least, to have been included in the general description of the British Islands. This want of acquaintance with Ireland was also probably increased by the circumstance of its national independence, as it is well known that the victorious arms of the Romans had never penetrated into that distant Island, in consequence of which it was regarded as completely removed from the centre of civilization, and looked upon as a barbarous country by the other nations of Europe. Still, however, it appears from the statement of the Roman historian Tacitus, who wrote in the latter part of the 1st Century, that, in a commercial point of view, the harbours of Ireland were better known in his time than those of England, for he says that " the soil and climate of Ireland, and the disposition and habits of the people, differ not much from those of Britain, while the approaches to the country and its ports, are better known, through commercial intercourse and merchantmen."*

But though the Fathers are entirely silent as to the first preachers of the Gospel in Ireland, there are some general statements made by some of them, with reference to Britain, which may be extended to the sister Island, though it is not expressly mentioned by any one of them. For it is well known, and it has been clearly proved by Abp. Ussher*, that Ireland was reckoned among the ancients as one of the British Islands, even long before the commencement of the Christian Era. I need not again particularly quote the passages of the Fathers to which I referred in my former Lecture ; it is sufficient to mention that the principal testimonies of this nature are to be found in the

---

* Taciti Agricola, Cap. xxiv.
† Usserii Brit. Eccles. Antiq. p. 723. (4to. Dub. 1639.)

Works of Tertullian, Eusebius, and Chrysostom, who flourished respectively in the beginning of the 3rd, 4th, and 5th Centuries after Christ. When Tertullian says that "the parts of Britain, *inaccessible to the Romans*, are subject to Christ"*, it is evidently intimated that Christianity had extended, in his time, beyond the limits of Roman Britain, and therefore he has been understood by Bp. Stillingfleet† and others as alluding to the northern parts of Great Britain beyond Adrian's Wall, though some have supposed that he refers to that part of Britain which is now called by the name of Scotland, but Dr. Lanigan "believes that there can be little doubt, that Tertullian had also in view the inhabitants of Ireland."‡ And, in like manner, when Eusebius informs us that some of the first preachers of Christianity "crossed the Ocean to those called the *British Islands*"§, and further, when St. Chrysostom says that "Churches and altars have been erected in the *British Islands*||," and again, that the Scriptures were studied and expounded "even in the very *British Islands*"¶—these expressions, employed in the *plural* number, may properly be applied to the "lesser" as well as the "greater" Britain, as the two British Islands were distinguished from each other by ancient writers. These, then, are some *indirect testimonies*, which seem to imply that the Christian Faith was known in some parts of Ireland at an early period, and it is scarcely necessary to observe that these Ecclesiastical authors lived long before the time of St. Patrick's mission. Indeed, it can hardly be supposed, *from the very nature of the case*, that Ireland would have been entirely deprived of the light of the Gospel for so long a period, when we remember that Christianity had been successfully preached to the British people in the neighboring country for more than 250 years before St. Patrick's time—when it appears that there was frequent communication between Ireland and other countries at that time—and when we take into account the ardent zeal of the first Christian Missionaries, who, inspired with the love of Christ, would never lose an

---

* Tertull. Opp. Tom. II. p. 290. (Ed. Semler.)
† Stillingfleet's Orig. Brit. p. 50. (Ed. Lond. 1685.)
‡ Lanigan, Vol. I. p. 2.
§ Eusebii Demonst. Evang. Lib. III. Cap. vii. p. 112. (Par. 1628.)
|| S. Chrysostomi Opp. Tom. I. p. 575. (Ed. Ben.)
¶ Ibid. Tom. III. p. 71.

opportunity of fulfilling the great commission entrusted to them by their Divine Master, to "go into the whole world, and preach the Gospel to every creature."

It is not very surprising, however, that there is so much obscurity about the first introduction of Christianity into Ireland, when we recollect that there is much the same obscurity about the introduction of Christianity into France, Spain, England, and even some parts of Italy, as there were no Ecclesiastical historians in those early times to record the events relating to the rise and progress of the Christian Faith in different countries, and to transmit them to future generations. And it is very much to the credit of our ancient annalists, that none of them have attempted to trace the conversion of the Irish people to the Twelve Apostles, or of their immediate successors, and they have thus avoided the temptation, so common to other writers of this class, of mixing up uncertain traditions and fabulous legends with the genuine history of those events of which the origin is lost in the remote antiquity of the times in which they occurred.

There are, indeed, some Irish Christians whose names have been handed down to us, who flourished before the time of St. Patrick, but it must be observed that, though they were natives of Ireland, yet they were Irishmen residing in foreign countries on the Continent of Europe, and the accounts of them have been delivered to us by foreign writers, nor does it appear that any of them had received the knowledge of Christianity while they were yet living in their native land. One of these was Mansuetus, who is said to have been the first Bishop of Toul, in France, and was undoubtedly an Irishman, to which is added in some accounts, that he was a disciple of St. Peter the Apostle. "There is, however," as Dr. Lanigan remarks, "no sufficient authority to prove that he lived in the times of St. Peter, and it is more than probable, that his mission to Toul did not take place until late in the 4th Century, or perhaps, about the beginning of the 5th." His life was written by the Abbot Adso in the 10th Century, and it is remarkable that his biographer states the fact, that Ireland contained many Christian tribes in the times of Mansuetus. Calmet, the French Divine, maintains that Mansuetus was sent from Rome to Toul about the middle of the 4th Century, and Dr. Lanigan supposes that the circumstance of his having been sent there by the Church of Rome, gave rise to the subsequent tradition of his having been sent by St. Peter himself, whose name has been constantly applied to all his successors in the See of Rome. *

We have another remarkable instance of the same kind, though a very unfortunate one, in the case of Celestius, the disciple and assistant of the famous heresiarch Pelagius, in the beginning of the 5th Century. It is generally believed that Celestius was a native of Ireland, and this opinion is chiefly founded on two passages in the Writings of St. Jerome, one of the greatest Doctors of the Latin Church, in both of which he is supposed to refer to Celestius, whom he describes as an Irishman. St. Jerome, with all his sanctity and learning, was certainly not remarkable for elegance of language when attacking a theological adversary, and accordingly, in one of these passages, in speaking of Celestius, with reference to his personal appearance, as " a large and corpulent dog, of the Scottish (Irish) nation,"† while in the other passage, he says of him, that he "was a most stupid person, fattened up with Scottish (Irish) porridge."‡ It is true, indeed, that, as St. Jerome does not expressly name Celestius, some persons have thought that he is referring to Pelagius himself, but without entering into further particulars, it is clear from other testimonies, that Pelagius was not an Irishman, but a native of Britain; and thus it is a remarkable circumstance, that this heresy, which so long disturbed the peace of the Church, was originated and propagated by two natives of the British Islands. It may be added, that St. Augustine, in one of his Works against the Pelagians, bears a high testimony to the intellectual abilities of Celestus, as he acknowledges him to be a man of exceedingly acute genius.§ It appears that he left Ireland in early life, and entered a Monastery on the Continent though it is not known in what country. During this time his faith was sound and his piety unquestionable; but having afterwards met with Pelagius at Rome, he adopted his principles, which ultimately led to the denial of the doctrine of Original Sin, and of the necessity of divine grace, in the conversion of the soul to God.

---

* Lanigan, Vol. I. p. 3.
† S. Hieronymi Opp. Tom. IV. p. 925. (Ed. Ven. 1766.)
‡ Ibid. p. 835.
§ S. Augustini Opp. Tom. X. p. 433. (Ed. Ben.)

I shall refer to one other illustrious Irishman, who was distinguished as a Christian poet and theologian in those early times—I mean Sedulius, who has been the subject of various opinions as, to the place of his birth, and the precise time in which he lived. Ussher, Ware, Harris, and Lanigan think that there is satisfactory evidence to prove that he was born in Ireland, and he is generally supposed to have lived during some part of the 5th Century. It is a curious circumstance that his name is only the Latin form of the name of Shiel, which is well known to be still quite common in Ireland. And it has been remarked, that "some of the most beautiful Hymns that are read in the Church, have been taken from Sedulius' Poems *;" and thus it appears that some of those glorious songs of praise which are chanted in the service of the Catholic Church throughout the whole world, were the productions of an Irish Christian in the 5th Century.

But I must now proceed to speak of those Irish Ecclesiastics who lived and died in their native country in those ancient times. It has been stated by some writers that there were several Bishops in Ireland before the time of St. Patrick, or the arrival of any Missionaries from Rome, and there are four members of the Episcopal order who are particularly mentioned by name in this description—Ailbe of Emly, Declan of Ardmore, Ibar of Begery, and Kieran of Saigir. It has been clearly shown, however, that there is no real foundation for the high antiquity which has thus been assigned to them, and though the three first of them were partly contemporary with St. Patrick, yet the last of them belongs to a much later period, as he flourished about the 6th Century of the Christian Era. St. Ailbe is said to have been born at Eliach in Munster, and according to several ancient accounts, he was ordained priest by St. Patrick himself. The Annals of Ulster and Innisfallen mark his death at the year 527, which is decisive evidence against the very early date of his ministry. Declan is said to have been the son of Erc, a prince in the County of Waterford, and was probably born in the latter part of the 5th Century. Ibar is said to have been a native of Ulster, and to have been one of the disciples of St. Patrick. He resided chiefly in his Monastery in Begery or Bege-

* Lanigan, Vol. I. p. 19,

rin, which means " little Ireland," and is a small Island near the harbour of Wexford. His death is placed in the ancient Irish Annals at the year 500*.

On the whole, then, it appears that there is no sufficient authority for the opinion, that there existed a Christian Hierarchy in Ireland before the mission of the first Catholic Bishop from Rome. There can be no doubt that there were Christians, and Christian Priests in the country before that period, and especially in the southern parts of Ireland, but there is no evidence to prove that there were any Bishops, and these Priests must therefore have been ordained in foreign countries. Their situation, in this respect, was probably similar to that of the Catholics in the United States, who had no resident Bishop among them until the latter end of the last Century, as the first Bishop of Baltimore, the oldest See in the great Republic, was not consecrated till the year 1790 ; though there were 20 Priests and a considerable body of the Catholic Laity in the country before that time†.

But I must now proceed to give some account of the first Missionary Bishop who was sent by authority of the See of Rome, to the people of Ireland, for the propagation of the Gospel, and the government of the Church, in that country. The individual who was selected for this commission was Palladius, who is supposed to have been a native of Britain, and who had held the office of Deacon, or, as some writers have called him, Archdeacon of the Roman Church, and had already been distinguished for his exertions in extirpating the Pelagian heresy from Britain. For it is recorded in St. Prosper's Chronicle, at the year 429, that " at the suggestion of Palladius the Deacon, Pope Celestine sends Germanus Bishop of Auxerre, in his own stead, in order that, having vanquished the heretics, he might direct the Britons to the Catholic Faith."‡

We shall now examine the celebrated passage of Prosper, relative to the mission of Palladius. It is expressed in these words—" Palladius is ordained and sent by Pope Celestine as the first Bishop to the Scots believing in Christ." The same account is repeated, nearly in the same words, by the Venerable Bede, both in his " History" and in his

---

* Lanigan, Vol. I. pp. 22–33.

† Metropolitan Catholic Almanac for U. S. (1859.) pp. 50, 251.

‡ S. Prosperi Chron. (Inter S. Aug. Opp. Tom. X. p. 128. App.)

" Chronicle."[*] Here it is necessary to explain that all learned men are fully agreed that by the " Scots" are meant the ancient inhabitants of Ireland. This may appear, indeed, quite a paradoxical opinion to those who are only acquainted with the modern names of those countries, but it has been conclusively proved by Archbishop Ussher that the name of " Scotia" or " Scotland" was invariably applied by ancient writers, not to the country which is now called by that name but to Ireland ; and that there is not a single instance of any other application of the name from the 4th to the 11th Century[†]. Without going into details, it is sufficient to refer to the fact, well known to all antiquarians, that the Scots originally came over from Spain and settled in Ireland at a very early period, and probably long before the beginning of the Christian Era ; that from thence the name of " Scotia" was gradually given to the country, in addition to that of Hibernia, by which it was formerly known, and that having afterwards passed over into Albania, the same name was, in process of time, applied to the new country, which is now exclusively known by the name of Scotland. But while this is now universally admitted, some writers have found a difficulty in reconciling the statement of Prosper with their own particular theories on this subject. Thus Archbishop Ussher, who was inclined to the opinion that there were Bishops in Ireland at an earlier period, endeavors to explain the word " primus" or " first" by supposing that it may refer to the circumstance of Palladius having been the *first sent* of the *two Bishops* appointed by Celestine for Ireland, of whom St. Patrick was the second in point of *time*—or that it may mean the *chief* Bishop in point of *dignity*, in the sense of Primate or Metropolitan.[‡] But both these are unusual senses of the word, and there is nothing whatever in the context to justify such an interpretation, as Prosper never mentions the name of St. Patrick at all, nor does he refer to any *other* Bishops, in comparison with Palladius.

Further, this testimony is of great importance in another point of view, because it proves that there were Christians in Ireland before the time of Palladius, as he is said to have been sent not merely for the *conversion* of the Irish, but to those who already " *believed in Christ*,"

* Bedæ Hist. Eccl. Angl. Lib. I. Cap. xlii. and Chron. ad an. 430.

† Usserii Brit. Eccles. Antiq. p. 725.

‡ Usser. Brit. Eccles. Antiq. p. 800.

which clearly implies that they were believers in Christ *before* his arrival in the country. An objection, indeed, has been founded upon a passage in Nennius, an ancient British Historian, in which he says—"Palladius was sent as Bishop first by Celestine, Pope of Rome, to the Scots who were *to be converted to Christ.*"* From this it might be inferred, that his mission was merely to a land of heathens, who had previously no knowledge of Christianity. But, even if these words be genuine, there is no comparison between the credit due to the authority of Prosper and of Nennius, as the former lived some Centuries before the latter, and in the very times to which his Chronicle refers, with the best opportunities of knowing the true state of Christianity in Ireland, as he was himself Secretary to the Pope. Still less credit is due to Platina, in his "Lives of the Popes," written more than 1000 years after the time, in which he says that Celestine " sent to the Scots, *desiring the Faith of Christ,* Palladius, whom he himself had created Bishop."† Indeed, it may be observed that the previous existence of Christianity seems to be implied in a remarkable passage in St. Patrick's own " Confession" (which is admitted to be a genuine document) in which he says to the Irish people—"I travelled in every direction for your sakes, amidst many dangers, even to remote places to which no person had ever come *to baptize, or ordain Clergymen,* or to confirm the people in the Faith‡"—which seems to intimate that there were *other* places *less remote* which had been visited by Christian missionaries before his time. It is also mentioned in one of the ancient Lives of St. Patrick, that in coming to a place near the river Shannon, where Palladius had never been, he found an altar and its sacred vessels for the celebration of the holy Sacrifice, which is a further incidental proof of the same point.

But there is also another important statement of Prosper, in which he speaks of the spiritual benefits conferred upon Ireland by Pope Celestine, so that he does not hesitate to say, that by his instrumentality Ireland was become a Christian country. After referring to the successful efforts of this Pope to preserve the purity of the Faith in Britain, he draws a comparison between his exertions for each of

* Nennii Hist. Brit. Cap. 53. (Apud Usser. p. 812.)

† Platinæ Vit. Pont. ad Celest. (Ed. Nurembergæ, 1481.)

S. Patricii Opuscula p. 206. (Ed. Dub. 1835.)

the two British Islands, when he adds that "having ordained a Bishop for the Scots, while he is anxious to preserve a *Roman Island Catholic*, he made also a *barbarous Island Christian*."* I need hardly explain, that the former of these means Britain, and the latter Ireland. On this passage Dr. Lanigan remarks—"I hope none of my countrymen will be offended at the epithet *barbarous*, here given by Prosper to Ireland. Whatever country did not form a part of the Roman Empire was so called at that period."† And it must be confessed, indeed, that the description was properly applicable to the Irish people at that time, who were generally in a state of heathenism and barbarism. There is a curious passage in the Writings of St. Jerome on this subject, which for the honor of our country, we might hope is exaggerated, though we can hardly question the veracity of the Saint. He says—" When I was a young man in Gaul, I saw the Scots (Irish), a British nation, *feeding on human flesh*"—and he goes on to give some shocking instances of this barbarous practice, after which he includes the whole nation in one sweeping sentence on another charge, when he adds that " the nation of the Scots (Irish), *have no wives of their own*," and live in utter neglect of the law of marriage‡. It must be remembered that St. Jerome lived shortly before the time of St. Patrick, and therefore it is some consolation to think that he is not speaking of *Christian* Ireland, but of a time when the nation was comparatively in a heathen state. In the second of the ancient Lives of St. Patrick, the mission of St. Palladius is thus briefly mentioned—" The most blessed Pope Celestine ordained Palladius, Archdeacon of the Roman Church, as Bishop, and sent him into the Island of Ireland, having delivered to him some relics of SS. Peter and Paul and other Saints, and also the books of the Old and New Testament."* This, indeed, is a point about which there can be no controversy, that whatever may have been the origin of Christianity in Ireland in the earliest times, *the first Christian Bishop was sent to Ireland by the successor of St. Peter in the See of Rome.*

After his consecration, Palladius set out for Ireland, accompanied by some Missionaries, four of whom are mentioned by name in some of

---

* S. Prosp. contra Collat. (Inter S. Aug. Opp. Tom. X. p. 195. App.)
† Lanigan, Vol. I. p. 42.
‡ S. Hieron. Opp. Tom. I. col. 503. (Ed. Par. 1609.)

St. Patrick's Lives, as Sylvester, Solonius, Augustine, and Benedict.
It is not particularly recorded where he landed, but from some indirect
allusions, it has been thought to be near the situation of the present
town of Wexford. Although he met with much opposition, yet it
appears that, according to the most authentic accounts, he baptized
several converts, and erected three Churches, which are generally supposed to have been situated in that part of the country which is now
called the County of Wicklow. But the mission of Palladius was of
short duration, and his success was comparatively small, in accordance with an old Irish adage, that " not to Palladius, but to Patrick,
did God grant the conversion of Ireland." The prince of the territory
ordered him to quit the country, and accordingly he was obliged to
withdraw, though he left some of his companions behind him, in order
to carry on the mission in his absence. He sailed from Ireland in the
latter part of the same year in which he arrived, and, after a stormy
passage, he landed in Britain, with the intention of proceeding to
Rome, and he is generally said to have died shortly afterwards, at a place
called Fordun, in the country of the Picts, or in modern Scotland†.

We have now arrived at the most remarkable period in the ancient
history of the Irish Church, when it pleased Almighty God to effect
the general conversion of the people of Ireland to the Christian Faith
by the ministry of St. Patrick. But, before I proceed to this subject,
it may be proper to make a few remarks, in refutation of an extraordinary opinion which has been advanced in modern times, with reference to this illustrious Saint. The opinion to which I refer is simply
this, that *there never was such a person in existence !* Now there have
been some writers who entertained doubts as to the precise *time* in
which he lived, or the reality of the *miracles* attributed to him, but it
does not appear that any author ever ventured to deny the very
existence of St. Patrick until the latter end of the last Century, when
Dr. Edward Ledwich, a Protestant Divine, published a large book
with the imposing title of " The Antiquities of Ireland", in which he
seriously maintained, with great appearance of learning, that the
popular belief on this point was entirely derived from uncertain traditions of the Middle Ages, and had no real foundation in the authen-

* Lanigan, Vol. I. p. 41.
† Ibid. Vol. I. pp. 37–47.

tie records of history. His principal arguments consist of two assertions, the one founded on the *supposed silence* of the most ancient writers, and the other on the *fictitious miracles* which had been ascribed to the Saint. Dr. Ledwich says—" It is an undoubted fact, that St. Patrick is not mentioned by any author, or in any work of veracity, in the 5th, 6th, 7th or 8th Centuries,''* and accordingly he concludes that his name is first mentioned about the middle of the 9th Century. Now this statement can only be supported by ignorance, or misrepresentation. In fact, there is no truth whatever in it. It is contradicted by the original works of St. Patrick, and the Canons which bear his name, the genuineness of which documents is admitted by the most learned Protestants. It is contradicted by the Alphabetical Hymn in honor of St. Patrick, written by Secundinus during the lifetime of the Saint. It is contradicted by the Irish Hymn or metrical account of St. Patrick, attributed to Fiech, which was probably written in the 6th Century. It is contradicted by the Paschal Epistle of Cummian, written, according to Ussher, in the year 634, and in which St. Patrick is expressly mentioned by name. It is contradicted even by the public Services of the Church used at that period, as, for instance, in an Anglo-Saxon Litany of the 7th Century, which contains the name of St. Patrick. It is contradicted by Adamnan's Life of St. Columbkill, written in the 7th Century, which also alludes to St. Patrick by name. It is contradicted by the evidence of an ancient MS. now in the British Museum, and which Ussher supposed to have been written in the beginning of the 8th Century, and which has since been published in the two great Collections of British Councils, by Spelman, and by Wilkins. Finally, it is contradicted by the testimony of the Venerable Bede, in the 8th Century, in whose Martyrology the Festival of St. Patrick in Ireland is marked at the 17th of March. Surely, then, we may justly adopt the conclusion of the learned Dr. O'Conor, who says that " even if all these authorities and Manuscripts in which St. Patrick is mentioned, were destroyed, the laws of just criticism forbid that after the lapse of so many ages, and the destruction of so many Monasteries and Libraries as formerly existed in Ireland before the Danish Invasions, the silence alone of such authors as remain (supposing such silence) should be admitted in evidence to

---

* Ledwich's Antiquities of Ireland, p. 375. (4to. Dub. 1790.)

overthrow a national tradition, so universal in every part of Ireland, Scotland, and Man, so immemorial, and so incorporated as that of St. Patrick is, with the traditionary usages, names, anniversaries, monastic ruins, and popular manners of one hundred millions of Irishmen who have existed since his time."* It is evident, then, that there is scarcely a single character recorded in sacred or profane history, of whose existence we have more clear and unequivocal evidence, than that of St. Patrick, and surely nothing can be more unreasonable than to argue that, because there is some uncertainty as to various *particulars* in his life, *therefore* there is no truth in *any part* of the narrative of his life. And yet the learned Antiquarian, to whom I refer, has urged an objection to the existence of St. Patrick, founded on the variety of opinions relative to the place of his birth, from which he comes to the conclusion, *that he was never born at all!* And as to the *miracles* of St. Patrick, the reality of such acts of divine interposition may be established by incontrovertible evidence, and it is surely in perfect accordance with the promises of the Divine Founder of the Church, as well as the exigencies of the mission in which he was engaged. Indeed it is fully admitted by several impartial Protestant historians, as for instance, the learned Jeremy Collier, who, after mentioning the fact, that " the writers of St. Patrick's Lives report a great many miracles performed by him," adds this remark—"neither have we reason to wonder at St. Patrick's being furnished with such a supernatural assistance, considering the difficulties of the task, and the barbarity of the people he had to deal with."† At the same time, it must be observed that there is a wide difference between the *true* miracles which the Almighty was pleased to perform by him, and those *spurious* and *ridiculous* miracles which have been ascribed to him by some superstitious writers of later times, and which have chiefly contributed to bring discredit and contempt upon the whole history of his life among those who are unable to distinguish between the genuine accounts of ancient authors, and the fabulous stories of modern compilers. Indeed, these very miracles, however false, instead of disproving his existence, strongly attests the contrary, for, as it has been justly remarked " miracles would never have been ascribed ex-

---

* Columbanus ad Hibernos, No. 3, p. 59. (Lond. 1310.)
† Collier's Eccles. Hist. Vol. I. p. 51. (Lond. 1707.)

cept to one who was already known in the traditions of the country,"* and accordingly we find that it was not for several Centuries after the death of St. Patrick, that the great multitude of miracles connected with his name were invented and published in the Lives of the Saint, which are still in circulation. It is well known that a great number of such biographies have been written at various times and by different persons. It is said that several of these were drawn up by the immediate disciples of St. Patrick, which have been lost in the course of time ; and we have the evidence of Joceline, the monk, who wrote his own account in the the 12th Century, that, in his time, not less than 66 different Tracts or Memoirs had been written concerning the Acts of St. Patrick, the greatest part of which were destroyed during the Danish persecution. However, it should be stated that seven of the most important of the ancient Lives of St. Patrick have been collected and published by John Colgan, an Irish Franciscan Friar, who lived in the 17th Century. The first and last of these were written in the Irish language, and the others in Latin. The oldest of them is called the Hymn of Fiech, because it is arranged in the form of poetry, and it is generally supposed to have been written in the 6th Century. Dr. Lanigan remarks of the second, third, and fourth of them, that " they are full of fables, and seem to have been copied, either from each other, or from some common repository, in which those stories had been collected."† The fifth Life is attributed to Probus, an Irishman, and is regarded as a very valuable Work, though, in the opinion of the best judges, it is not older than the 10th Century. The sixth is that of Joceline, a Welshman, who lived in the 12th Century, and was brought over to Ireland in the time of Henry II. It is one of the most celebrated of the Lives of St. Patrick, though Dr. Lanigan pronounces it to be the worst of them all. The seventh is the longest of these biographies, and is considered to be a very useful Work. It is distinguished as the " Tripartite Life," because it is divided into three parts, and the date of its composition is generally assigned to the 10th Century. These Works, together with the Writings of St. Patrick himself, and some occasional allusions to his history in other ancient documents, form the principal materials from

---

* King's Church Hist. of Ireland, Vol. I. p. 14. (3rd Ed.)
† Lanigan, Vol. I. p. 84.

which all the modern Lives of the Saint have been compiled, though it must be confessed that it is a task of considerable difficulty to arrange and harmonize these different narratives, and to deduce a consistent and authentic account from the combined testimony of them all, in chronological order.

But it is time to enter into some particulars of the life and ministry of the Apostle of Ireland—and first, with reference to the time and place of his birth. *Where* was St. Patrick born? This is a question which has been variously answered, according to the fanciful attempts of different writers to identify the places mentioned in his Lives with the corresponding names of localities in modern countries. According to these conjectures, it has been held by some, that he was born in Cornwall in England—by others, in Pembrokeshire in Wales—and by others, (which is the most unfounded of all), in some part of Ireland itself. The most general opinion, since the time of Ussher and Colgan in the 17th Century, has been, that his native place was Kilpatrick in Scotland, which is situated between Dumbarton and Glasgow; but, after all, this opinion rests on very slight grounds, which I shall endeavor briefly to explain. The Hymn of Fiech says that he was born in a place called Nemthur. But no one ever heard of such a place in any of the three kingdoms. However, an ancient commentator on the Hymn of Fiech informs us, that Nemthur was a town in North Britain, afterwards called Alcluit, which is now known by the name of Dumbarton. But this seems to have been a mere conjecture, advanced without any historical authority. Subsequently, it appears, that Jocelino distinguished Nemthur from Alcluit, and Ussher, following his account, supposes that it was the same with the modern town of Kilpatrick. Such is the principal evidence in favor of this opinion. Let us now attend to the statement of St. Patrick himself, in the following passage in his "Confession." He says—"My father was Calpornius, a Deacon, son of Potitus, a Presbyter, of the town of Benaven Taberniæ. He had near the town a small villa called Enon, where I was carried into captivity."[*] We may reasonably suppose, then, that he was born in the place where his father lived; but the difficulty is, to fix those places with precision in modern geography. There were no such places known in Scotland, so as to reconcile St. Patrick's own account

---

[*] S. Patricii Opuscula. p. 184.

with the opinion of Kilpatrick being his native place. Accordingly there is another opinion which has been held by many learned men, and especially by Dr. Lanigan, who has fully discussed the whole question in a most elaborate examination of ancient authorities. His opinion is, that St. Patrick was born in France, and that the name of Benaven Taberniæ is the same as the present town of Boulogne-sur-mer in Picardy. It has been shown that, in the 4th Century, that town was generally known by the name of Bononia, which was only the *Latin* form of the *Celtic* name of Benaven, given to it by St. Patrick—and the name Tabernia, or Tarvenna, was the ancient name of the district in which this town was situated, while it is probably added to the other, in order to distinguish it from the City of Bononia, or Bologna, in Italy. This opinion is confirmed by the ancient traditions of the inhabitants of that country, and it is the only one that fully agrees with all the geographical and historical allusions in the accounts of his life. With respect to the name of Nemthur, mentioned as his birth-place by Fiech, it appears to be the name of a country or province well known at that time, including the territory of Boulogne ; and accordingly we find that Probus expressly asserts that Benaven, the birth-place of the Saint, was undoubtedly in the Province of Nevtria, which was the Latin name of this place. It must be remarked, however, that Probus calls St. Patrick, a Briton, and he himself seems to intimate the same thing, when he speaks of being with his parents in Britain*. But here it must be observed that there was another Britain in France, as well as that which is now called Great Britain, and it is expressly mentioned by the Venerable Bede, that the Island of Britain derived its name from the Britons who came from the Armorican district on the Continent, and settled in the country†, and thus there can be no doubt that the ancient Britons in England were originally colonists from Britannia in France, while the name of Britain still continued to be applied to the continental territory, even at a later age than that of St. Patrick. Indeed there is a remarkable passage in the ancient life of the Saint by Probus, in which France is evidently mentioned as St. Patrick's country, though he lived at a time when the name of Britain was exclusively applied to England :

---

* S. Patricii Opuscula, p. 194.

† Bedæ Hist. Eccles. Angl. Lib. I. Cap. i.

for he writes that on the Saint's endeavoring to escape from Ireland, a man sold him to be carried *into Gaul*, and that the sailors brought him to his *own country*, and landed him at Bourdeaux in France*.

We shall now briefly consider the other question— *When* was St. Patrick born? I shall mention at once a satisfactory mode of ascertaining this point, founded on a remarkable passage in his own " Confession." It appears that, when he had determined on preaching the Gospel in Ireland, and was about to be consecrated Bishop for that mission, a certain person who had long·been his friend, publicly accused him of some fault which he had committed when a foolish boy scarcely 15 *years old*. Now, though he had confessed this fault before he was ordained a Deacon, yet he says that *after* 30 *years*, his friend, to whom he had communicated it in the bitterness of his sorrow, came forward to expose him in this manner, and to prevent his admission into the Episcopal order† It is evident, then, that those 30 years must be counted back from the time when the fault was committed to the time of his consecration, and if we add the 15 years of his age to that time, we shall come to the conclusion, that he was 45 years old when he was made Bishop. But that event certainly took place in the year 432, from which subtracting 45, we shall have the year 387 as the date of his birth, and this is now generally admitted to be the most probable opinion. According to Ficch's Hymn and some of the ancient Lives, his first name was Succath, and he is said by several respectable authors to have received the name of Patrick from Pope Celestine, on the occasion of his mission to Ireland. But there seems to be no sufficient authority for this statement, as it rests entirely on the statement of the old Scholiast in Ficch's Hymn, and the Saint never speaks of himself under any other name than that of Patrick, though there is no reason to doubt that he had also the name of Succath, which, according to the Scholiast, was given him by his parents at his baptism.

The first remarkable event in the life of St. Patrick was his captivity, which took place, according to his own account, in the 16th year of his age, and therefore in the year of our Lord 403. He was carried away from his native land by some Irish pirates, probably under the

---

* Lanigan, Vol. I. pp. 88-128.
† S. Patricii Opuscula, p. 196.

command of the renowned Niall of the Nine Hostages, King of Ire-
lan, and sold as a slave in the North of Ireland to a certain Pagan,
whose name was Milcho. The Saint himself, with the most profound
humility, acknowledges this event to be a just punishment from God on
account of the sins of himself and his countrymen who were involved in
the same calamity with him. He says—" I was ignorant of the true
God, and I was brought into Ireland in captivity, along with so many
thousands of persons, according to what we deserved, because we departed from God, and kept not his precepts, and were disobedient to
our Priests, who pointed out to us the way of salvation ; and the Lord
brought upon us the anger of his indignation, and scattered us among
many nations, even to the ends of the earth."* The part of Ireland
in which he had to endure the hardships of slavery appears to have
been situated in the County of Antrim, near the present town of Bally-
mena, and in the vicinity of the mountain called Sliev Mis, where he
was employed in feeding the cattle of his master. But it pleased
Almighty God, in accordance with the usual operations of His grace
in the hearts of His elect people, to bless this season of affliction to his
spiritual sanctification, and he himself acknowledges it with deep gratitude to the Giver of every good and perfect gift. There is no doubt
that St. Patrick had been baptized in his infancy, and the seeds of divine grace had been sown in his heart from his earliest years, but as yet
they had not produced the fruits of holiness in his life. And it may
be here remarked, that this circumstance is totally inconsistent with
the foolish stories of Joceline and others, about the miracles performed
by St. Patrick when a boy, of which, however, there is no account
whatever in the most ancient and authentic Lives of the Saint. We
have now reached the great turning point in the spiritual history of
St. Patrick, which we do not hesitate to describe as the conversion of
his soul to God. It does not appear to have been effected by any
human instrumentality whatever—it was the immediate work of the
Holy Spirit in his heart, convincing him of his sins, and applying to
him the lessons of Christian truth which he had learned in his childhood. He was, indeed, placed in peculiar and extraordinary circumstances, living among heathens, deprived of the opportunity of enjoy-
ing the benefits of the Christian Ministry and the Christian Sacraments:

S. Patricii Opuscula, p. 184.

and he found by his own happy experience, that affliction is the School of the Saints, in which God trains up His children for grace here, and for glory hereafter. But let us hear his own simple and touching narrative. "I was not from my childhood a believer in the only God, but continued in death and in unbelief until I was severely chastened, and in truth I have been humbled by hunger and nakedness, and it was my lot to travel se Ireland every day sore against my will, until I was almost exhausted. But this proved rather a benefit to me, because by means of it I have been corrected by the Lord, and he has fitted me for being this day what was once far from me, so that I should interest myself about the salvation of others, when I used to have no such thoughts even for myself."[*] Again, he says of this period—"The Lord brought me to a sense of the unbelief of my heart, that I might even at a late season call my sins to remembrance, and turn with all my heart to my Lord, who regarded my low estate, and taking pity on my youth and ignorance, watched over me before I knew Him, or had sense to discern between good and evil, and comforted me, as a father doth his son. Wherefore I cannot be silent, nor is it right that I should pass over such benefits, and such grace which the Lord was pleased to bestow upon me in the land of my captivity."[†] Thus he was, by an act of perfect contrition, reconciled to God, and he thankfully records the mercy of God to his soul. "I know this most certainly, that before I was humbled, I was like a stone that lies in the deep mire, and He who is mighty came, and in His mercy raised me up, and set me upon the top of a wall. And therefore I am bound to make some return to the Lord for so great benefits, both here and in eternity, which the human mind cannot conceive."[‡] Once more, he thus describes his own devotional exercises at this period—"After I had come to Ireland, I was employed every day in feeding cattle, and frequently in the day I was in the habit of praying, and the love of God was thus growing stronger and stronger, and His fear and faith were increasing in me, so that in a single day I would say as many as a hundred prayers, and in the night almost as many. And I used to remain in the woods, too, and on the mountain, and would rise for prayer before daylight,

---

[*] S. Patricii Opuscula, p. 196.

[†] Ibid. p. 185.

[‡] Ibid. p. 188.

in the midst of snow, ice, and rain, and I received no injury from it, nor was there any sloth in me, as I now see, for then the spirit was fervent within me."[*]

St. Patrick's captivity lasted six years, according to his own "Confession" and Fiech's Hymn, and thus we may fix the date of its termination to the year 409. He says he was informed in his sleep, that the time of his liberation had arrived. "At night I heard a voice saying to me, *Thou fastest well, and art soon to go to thine own country.* And again after a little time I heard an answer saying to me, *Behold! a ship is ready for you.* And the ship was not near, but about 200 miles off, and in a place where I had never been, nor was acquainted with any one."[†] Accordingly he betook himself to flight, and obtained a passage with some difficulty, and sailed from a port in the South of Ireland, and arrived at the end of his voyage in three days. It appears, however, from his own narrative, that the Saint and his companions were wandering for 28 days through a desert country, before he reached home. It was at this time that a remarkable circumstance occurred, which throws some light on the religious practices of St. Patrick, and of the Christian Church in his time. He says that "one night, while I was asleep, Satan tempted me dreadfully, which I shall remember as long as I live. For he fell upon me like a great rock, and took away all the strength of my limbs. But I know not how it happened that I invoked Elias in spirit, and during this time I saw the sun rising in the heavens, and while I was calling Elias! Elias! with all my might, behold the splendor of that sun relieved me of all my burden, and I believe I was assisted by Christ my Lord, and His Spirit was at that very time crying out in my behalf."[‡] It is scarcely necessary to remark here, that whatever degree of obscurity there may be in this passage, it seems clearly to intimate that the Invocation of Saints was regarded by St. Patrick as a pious and salutary practice.

St. Patrick was now 22 years of age, and it was probably shortly after this time that he entered the celebrated Monastery, or College, of St. Martin of Tours, who is said by some writers to have been his

[*] S. Patricii Opuscula, p. 190.
[†] Ibid. p. 190.
[‡] Ibid. 192.

uncle by his mother's side. Here he remained four years, during which he was engaged in prosecuting the studies of a Christian education, though he never entered any of the Monastic orders; and at the conclusion of this period he returned to his friends, and, as the Rheims Breviaries state, applied himself most fervently to the practice of piety. It was about this time that he had the misfortune to fall into a second captivity, from which, however, he was liberated after 60 days; and on his return home, his parents requested him not to leave them any more, after all the hardships he had undergone. But Almighty God had a glorious work for him to do, and He was preparing him for it by all the trials and difficulties of his former life, as well as by a previous course of long study and prayer. It was at this time that he had a remarkable Vision, which probably decided the future course of his life, as well as the future destinies of the Irish Church. He thus relates it in his own Confession—" I saw in a vision of the night a person named Victricius coming as if from Ireland with innumerable letters, and he gave me one of them, and I read the beginning of the letter, running thus, *The voice of the people of Ireland;* and as I was reading the commencement of the letter, I thought at that very moment that I heard the voice of those who were near the wood of Focluth, which is adjoining to the Western Sea, and they cried out thus, as it were with one voice, *We entreat thee, holy youth, to come and walk still among us,* and I was very much affected to the heart, and could read no further, and so I awoke." " Thanks be to God," he adds, " that after many years, the Lord hath granted to them according to their cry." Yet it does not seem that St. Patrick fully understood the import of this communication at the time, as we find that he still remained several years in his own country. It appears that he spent nine years in a Collegiate institution in the Island of Lerins in the Tuscan Sea, and four years under the instruction of the celebrated St. Germanus, Bishop of Auxerre, while preparing for the duties of the Ecclesiastical life. It has been stated, also, on the authority of some ancient writers, that he accompanied Germanus and Lupus on their mission to Britain, to oppose the Pelagian heresy, in the year 429. It is very possible that this statement may be correct, though it is not mentioned by the oldest authorities; and it may be here remarked, that if ever St. Patrick was in England at any period of his life, it must have been either on this occasion, or in the course of his own progress to the Irish mission three years afterwards, as it is certain that from the time of his arrival in Ireland as a missionary Bishop, he never left that country till the day of his death.

We have already referred · to the appointment of Palladius as the first Bishop in Ireland, by authority of Pope Celestine, in the year 431, and it was probably in the latter part of the same year that St. Patrick was sent to Rome by St. Germanus, with a recommendation to the Pope as a fit person to be employed in the Irish mission, of which Palladius had already been appointed the chief. Accordingly it is stated in some of the Lives of the Saint, that he was approved of by Pope Celestine, received his benediction, and was empowered by him to proceed to Ireland, as principal assistant to Palladius, a situation which was nearly equivalent to that of coadjutor and successor, though he was not yet invested with the Episcopal dignity. It is true that he did not set out from Rome with Palladius, because it is probable that he did not arrive there till after the departure of Palladius, and also because he obtained permission to visit his friends in France before he proceeded to Ireland. It is generally admitted by the best authorities, that St. Patrick was not consecrated Bishop at Rome by Celestine himself, and it is surprising to find that this admission is frequently quoted by Protestant writers as an argument against St. Patrick having received his authority from the Pope, as if the Pope himself *consecrated* every Bishop who was *appointed* by him to a foreign mission. But " it is easy to account for his not having been made Bishop at Rome, for Palladius was the person fixed upon as chief of the mission, and as the Bishop on that occasion; nor was it, or is it usual to send, on the commencement of a mission, more than *one* Bishop to any one country."* And thus we find that Pope Gregory the Great, in the end of the following Century, appointed at first but one Bishop, St. Augustine, for the mission of England; nor was he consecrated by the Pope himself, but by the Bishop of Arles, in France; and there is good reason to believe that St. Patrick was also consecrated in the same country, after his departure from Rome, on receiving intelligence of the death of Palladius. The account of St. Patrick's consecration by Celestine is not to be found in any of the Lives, except

* Lanigan, Vol. I. p. 191.

in the two most modern of them, from which it has been copied into some other documents; but his mission from Rome is not only stated by some of the most ancient authorities, but is generally admitted by the most respectable Protestant writers, and among others by Ussher[*], Cave[†], Collier[‡], and Milner[§]. These are all Protestant Divines of the Church of England, and to them I shall add the testimony of Mosheim, the learned Lutheran ecclesiastical historian. His statement is this— "Celestine, Bishop of Rome, sent into Ireland to spread Christianity among the barbarians of that Island, in the first place, Palladius, whose labors were not crowned with much success. After his death, *Celestine* sent Succathus, a Scotchman, whose name he changed to Patricius, into Ireland, in the year 432; a man of vigor, and, as appears from the event, not unfit for such an undertaking. He was far more successful in his attacks upon idolatry; and having converted many of the Irish to Christianity, he, in the year 472, established at Armagh the See of an Archbishop of Ireland. Hence St. Patrick, although there were some Christians in Ireland before his day, has been justly called the Apostle of Ireland, and the Father of the Irish Church, and is held in high veneration to this day."[||] It may be remarked also, that the Irish Nobles, in their Letter to Pope John XXII., refer to the fact, that " our chief Apostle and Patron, St. Patrick, was commissioned by your predecessor Pope Celestine, according to the inspiration of the Holy Ghost"[¶]—while the highest of all authorities, the Roman Missal, in the Collect for St. Patrick's day, ascribes the mission of the Saint to the Almighty Himself, " who vouchsafed to send the blessed Patrick, Confessor and Bishop, to preach His glory to the Gentiles"[* *].

At length, then, we have come to St. Patrick's arrival in Ireland, which took place, according to the Irish Annals, in the 1st year of the Pontificate of Sixtus III. who succeeded Pope Celestine on the 28th April, 432. The place where he landed is generally supposed to have

---

* Usser. Antiq. p. 1100.

† Cave, Script. Eccles. Tom. I. p. 332. (Lond. 1688.)

‡ Collier's Eccles. Hist. Vol. I. p. 51.

§ Milner's Church Hist. Vol. II. p. 369.

|| Mosheim's Eccles. Hist. Vol. I. p. 416. (Lond. 1850.)

¶ King's Church Hist. p. 1120.

* * Miss. Rom. p. 421. (Dub. 1833.)

been in the harbour of Dublin, or according to others, in that of Wick-low. But this first attempt was unsuccessful, and in consequence of the opposition of the natives, he embarked again in the same vessel which brought him to Ireland, with the intention of visiting the former scene of his captivity. He landed on the shore of the County of Down, and probably near Strangford, where he had the opportunity of preaching the Gospel, and receiving the first Irish converts into the Church of Christ. Among these was the prince of the territory, named Dicho, who believed and was baptized with all his family, and who showed his zeal for the propagation of the faith by the grant of a place for the celebration of divine worship. This Church is commonly known by the name of Patrick's Barn, and was probably nothing more than a real barn, belonging to Dicho, which was fitted up for religious purposes. This was the first Church errected by St. Patrick in Ireland. It was situated in the place now called Saul, and it is a remarkable circumstance, that it was in this place that the Saint after-wards ended his days in peace, within a short distance of Downpatrick, where his mortal remains were interred. St. Patrick, after remaining here a short time, proceeded by land to the place where his old master lived in the County of Antrim, with the view of persuading him to embrace the Christian Faith. But Milcho was an obstinate heathen, and refused to hear the Word of God. The Saint, therefore, returned to Dicho, and continued to preach in that part of the country with great success. In the following year, St. Patrick had an opportunity of preaching the Gospel before King Leogaire, the supreme monarch of Ireland, and the assembled princes of the whole kingdom, at the royal palace of Tara, in Meath. This place is famous in the ancient Annals of Ireland, and is celebrated in one of the beautiful Melodies of our national Poet, in those well known verses on "The Harp that once t' rough Tara's Halls" &c. But the most important event that ever took place in the Halls of Tara, was the preaching of St. Patrick, on Easter Sunday, the 2nd of April, in the year 433. It appears that the Saint had arrived at Slane on the evening of Holy Saturday, and, according to the custom of the Christian Church, he made prepara-tions for celebrating the Festival of Easter by lighting the Paschal fire. But it happened at this very time that the king and the assembled princes were engaged in celebrating an idolatrous festival, of which fire worship formed an essential part. It was a standing law, that no fire should be kindled throughout the Province, until after the great fire should be lighted in the royal palace of Tara. St. Patrick's Paschal fire, however, was kindled before that of the palace, and being seen from the heights of Tara, excited great astonishment. On consulting the Magi, the King received this remarkable answer— "Unless yonder fire, which we see, be extinguished this night, it will never be extinguished; moreover, it will get the better of all our accustomed fires, and he, who has kindled it, will destroy your kingdom." On the next day, St. Patrick preached at the palace before the King and his nobles, and according to some accounts, the King himself was converted to Christianity, but this statement is not supported by the best authorities. Still, however, it appears that he continued to preach both in East and West Meath for some time, to erect Churches, and to ordain Clergymen in various parts of the country, where he probably continued for about two years.

The next scene of St. Patrick's labors was the Province of Connaught, where he is said to have remained for seven years, and to have met with the most extraordinary success in the conversion of the native heathen to the Christian Faith, and especially in that district whose inhabitants he had seen in the Vision, beseeching him to come and labour among them. Indeed some of the accounts speak of 12,000 converts, including seven of the native princes, having been baptized on one of these occasions; and we find that he himself speaks, in his "Confession", of several thousand persons having been baptized by him. Yet he was still frequently exposed to great personal dangers from the persecution of the Pagans, and in the course of his mission an attempt was made against his life by the heathen Magi, from which he was saved by the protection of the Almighty, and the interposition of some powerful friends. It was during this period that he is said to have retired, at the beginning of Lent, to a lofty mountain in Mayo, which is now called by the name of Croagh Patrick, to spend that holy time in fasting and prayer, and to meditate among its tranquil elevations, above the smoke and stir of heathen Ireland. And it may be remarked, that this was the occasion on which, according to a well known popular tradition, he is said to have expelled all the venomous reptiles out of Ireland, and to have pronounced against them sentence of perpetual banishment from the country. Joceline, the latest of his biographers, is the only one of them that has mentioned this circumstance. "To this place," he says, "he gathered together the several tribes of serpents and venomous creatures, and drove them headlong into the Western Ocean, and from thence proceeds that exemption which Ireland enjoys from all poisonous reptiles."* But it appears that Solinus, who wrote some hundred years before St. Patrick's arrival in Ireland, takes notice of this exemption, and among other proofs Colgan alleges, that in the most ancient documents of Irish history there is not the least allusion to venomous animals ever having been found in the country.

About the year 442, St. Patrick proceeded to the Province of Ulster, and preached in Tyrconnell, in the County of Donegal. The principal event which occurred here was the conversion of Owen, an Irish prince, from whom the Barony of Ennishowen derives its name—and his visit to the prince in the neighborhood of Derry. After this he made a missionary journey through the present Counties of Tyrone, Monaghan, Meath, Wicklow, Kildare, Queen's County, and Carlow, and thence proceeded to Munster, and arrived at Cashel, the usual residence of the ancient Kings of that Province. Ængus, who was afterwards King, was one of his first converts, and the Saint is said to have remained seven years in that Province, though few particulars of his mission have been recorded. After having solemnly bestowed his blessing on the people of Munster, he left that Province for Down, from which he proceeded to Louth and the adjoining parts of Ulster, where he probably continued about two years, and shortly afterwards founded the Cathedral Church and Archiepiscopal See of Armagh, about the year 455, after which he appears to have returned to his favorite retreat at Saul, and to have spent the remainder of his life between it and Armagh, in a state of comparative retirement.

In some modern Lives of St. Patrick, we have an account of his visit to Dublin, of the conversion and baptism of King Alphin and all his people in Patrick's Well, of the erection of a Church by him, on the foundation of which St. Patrick's Cathedral was afterwards built, and of his pronouncing his blessing upon Dublin, and predicting the future greatness of the city. But, unfortunately, there is not a word about any of these events in the authentic records of his life, as none of them

---

* Wills' Lives of Illustrious Irishmen, Vol. I p. 92.

can be traced to a higher antiquity than to the time of Joceline, in the 12th Century, and they are generally rejected by the most learned antiquarians. On the same authority, we have also an account of his going to Rome in his old age, in order to get the privileges of the new Metropolis of Armagh confirmed by the Holy See, and of his being decorated with the Pallium by the Pope, and appointed Papal Legate in Ireland. But, as Dr. Lanigan remarks, "this pretended tour to Rome, and the concomitant circumstances, are all set aside by the testimony of St. Patrick himself,"[*]—and as they rest upon no solid authority, they are not entitled to any degree of credit. Still more unfounded is the fable about St. Patrick's Purgatory, in Lough Derg, in the County of Donegal, which is never mentioned in any of the Lives of the Saint, and does not appear to have been heard of till the 11th Century. It was demolished in the year 1497, by order of Pope Alexander VI., but it has since been partially restored. No mention of it is allowed in any part of the Church Service, though it was once inserted in a Roman Breviary printed in 1522, but was omitted by authority in every subsequent edition. I need scarcely remark, that this name has reference entirely to the acts of penance performed by the pilgrims, and not to any state of purification in the world of spirits.

St. Patrick was at Saul when he was attacked with his last illness. He was anxious, indeed, to finish the course of his earthly pilgrimage in Armagh, where he had founded the Archiepiscopal See of Ireland, and accordingly he set out for that place, but was induced to return to Saul, in consequence, as it is said, of a supernatural direction which he received to that effect. Seven days after this, he resigned his soul into the hands of God, on the 17th of March, having been attended by Bishop Tassach, from whom he received the holy viaticum. With respect to the precise year in which he died, and his age at the time of his death, there has been much difference of opinion among his biographers; but probably the most satisfactory one is that of Dr. Lanigan, who, after a full review of all the evidence, comes to the conclusion, "that our Apostle was called to heaven, either at the age of 78 years, or in his 78th year, as his birth occurred in 387, and his death in 465."[†] There was indeed an old tradition, which has

* Lanigan, Vol. I. p. 319.
† Ibid. Vol. I. p. 363.

Leen adopted by many respectable authors, that the Saint lived to the extraordinary age of 120 years, and several fanciful points of comparison were drawn between him and Moses, founded on this supposed resemblance. Even the learned Archbishop Ussher held that St. Patrick died in the year 493, at the age of 120, and the whole system of his chronological calculations is founded on these two positions. But, without going into further details, as to the former point, it has been clearly ascertained that Benignus, his successor in the See of Armagh, died in the year 468, and as to the latter point, it has been shown to rest on no sufficient authority, and is totally irreconcileable with the most authentic facts of history. When the news of his death spread through the country, it is stated in Fiech's Hymn, that " the Clergy of Ireland flocked from all quarters to celebrate his funeral obsequies," which were performed by a constant succession of services, consisting not only in the celebration of Mass, but also in Psalmody and the chanting of Hymns, night and day, accompanied by an extraordinary profusion of torches and lights, and the funeral service is said to have been continued in this manner for twelve days. His body was interred in Downpatrick, though some of his relics were brought to Armagh, and hence, St. Bernard, in his Life of St. Malachy, says that St. Patrick presided over Armagh in his life, and rests in it after his death*. It is well known, that the remains of St. Patrick are now deposited with those of the two other great Patron Saints of Ireland, St. Bridget, and St. Columbkill, the former of whom died in the early part and the latter in the end, of the 6th century. St. Bridget had been buried in Kildare, and St. Columbkill in Iona, but their bodies had been subsequently removed to Down, and finally a solemn translation of the relics to a more sacred part of the Church took place in the year 1186, in the presence of Cardinal Vivian, fifteen Bishops, and a great number of Ecclesiastics.

We may here briefly refer to the Writings attributed to St. Patrick, which have come down to our time. They are but few and short, and were first collected and printed at London in the year 1656. The most important of them is the document which I have frequently quoted, under the title of the " Confession" of St. Patrick. It is chiefly

---

* S. Bernardi Opp. Tom. II. p. 73. (Ed. Lyon. 1854.)

written in the form of a Letter to the Irish Christians, to express his gratitude to God for the singular mercies bestowed upon himself, and the people of Ireland by his instrumentality, and to confirm them in their holy faith by showing them that the Almighty had assisted him in an extraordinary manner for the purpose of effecting their conversion. It contains but few references to particular facts and events, and consequently throws but little light on the disputed portions of the history of his life and doctrines. It was probably composed shortly before his death, and it concludes with these words— "This is my Confession before I die." The next of his Works is his "Epistle to Coroticus," who, though apparently a professing Christian, was a tyrant and a pirate. He landed on the coast of the South of Ireland, during St. Patrick's visit to Munster, and began to plunder the district in which the Saint had just been engaged in baptizing and confirming a great number of converts, and, having murdered several of them, carried off others and sold them as slaves to the Picts and Scots. St. Patrick wrote that Letter on this occasion, denouncing as excommunicate those who had taken part in this expedition, and exhorting them to return to repentance. These, then, with a collection of Canons, are generally acknowledged by learned men to be the genuine Writings of the Saint; but there are some others, the authenticity of which is very doubtful. Such is the Treatise "on the Abuses of of the World," which has also been ascribed to St. Cyprian and to St. Augustine, and is printed among the spurious Works in the best editions of these Fathers. The Treatise "on the Three Habitations," which is generally included in St. Patrick's Works, has also been ascribed to St. Augustine, and is printed among his supposititious Works, while others have attributed it to St. Bernard, in the 12th Century, but the real author of it is entirely unknown.

I have thus endeavored to give a rapid sketch of the principal events in the life of that illustrious Prelate, who labored with such untiring zeal for the propagation of the Gospel in Ireland, and who is justly regarded with the highest degree of veneration, as the Father of the Irish Church. It is well remarked by a Protestant author of the present day, that "St. Patrick was an earnest preacher of the Gospel, pious, energetic, and full of zeal. His mind would appear to have been deeply imbued with the love of monastic institutions and of the eremetic life. He was neither a learned Divine nor a pleasing writer, if it be fair to judge from the Works attributed to him ; but he was a sincere and holy Bishop in the Church of God, who performed the work of an Evangelist in all honesty amongst the people of his adoption, and committed to the Church (in the foundation of which he had so great a part) the same tradition of the faith as he had himself received from his Christian forefathers."* And I cannot forbear to quote here the excellent remarks of the pious Father Butler, in his valuable Work on the " Lives of the Saints," with reference to the spiritual character of St. Patrick. " The Apostles of nations were all interior men, endowed with a sublime spirit of prayer. The salvation of souls being a supernatural end, the instruments ought to bear a proportion to it, and preaching proceed from a grace which is supernatural. To undertake this holy function without a competent stock of sacred learning, and without the necessary precautions of human prudence and industry, would be to tempt God. But sanctity of life, and the union of the heart with God, are a qualification far more essential than science, eloquence, and human talent. Many almost kill themselves with studying to compose elegant sermons, which flatter the ear, but reap very little fruit. Their hearers applaud their parts, but very few are converted. Most preachers now-a-days have learning, but are not sufficiently grounded in true sanctity and a spirit of devotion. Interior humility, purity of heart, recollection, and the spirit and the assiduous practice of holy prayer, are the principal preparation for the ministry of the Word, and the true means for acquiring the science of the Saints. A short devout meditation and fervent prayer, which kindles a fire in the affections, furnishes more thought proper to move the hearts of the hearers, and inspire them with sentiments of true virtue, than many years employed barely in reading and study. St. Patrick, and other Apostolic men, were dead to themselves and the world, and animated with the spirit of perfect charity and humility, by which they were prepared by God to be such powerful instruments of His grace, as, by the miraculous change of so many hearts, to plant in entire barbarous nations, not only the faith, but also the spirit of Christ."†

---

* Hook's Eccl. Biography, Vol. VII. p. 576.
† Butler's Lives of the Saints, (March 17.)

And now, I must proceed to make some observations on a very important subject, relative to the nature of the Christian doctrine held by the primitive Church of Ireland, with reference to the great controversies of the present day. It may be remarked that the same thing which has happened to the Catholic Church *in general*, has happened to the Irish Church *in particular*. It has been said that the ancient Irish Christians never acknowledged the Supremacy of the Pope, and that in all the principal articles of the Christian Faith, they held those doctrines which are now called Protestant, but that, in course of time, after a long and successful resistance, they were obliged at last to submit to the yoke of Rome, from which the national Church was emancipated at the period of the Reformation, and restored to its original independence and purity. Thus Abp. Usaher published a Work, in which he endeavors to prove that the religion of the ancient Irish Church, was substantially the same with that of the modern branch of the Church of England, established by law in that country*. Now, I think that he has satisfactorily shown, that the doctrines taught by the old Irish Divines, were substantially the same as those which are now held *in common by Protestants and Catholics;* but surely, this proves nothing on *either* side of the question, and I cannot find any conclusive evidence that they held any of those doctrines which are *peculiar to Protestants*, as distinguished from Catholics, while, on the other hand, I find conclusive evidence that they did hold several of those doctrines which are *peculiar to Catholics*, as distinguished from Protestants. And, in fact, the same argument from *prescription*, which has so justly been employed in defence of the divine origin of the Catholic Church, may be equally applied in favor of that branch of the Catholic Church which existed in Ireland before the period of the Protestant Reformation. We maintain that the Catholic Church is the only true Church of Christ, because she alone has preserved the *unity of the Christian Faith*, in uninterrupted succession, since the days of the Apostles; and while all other Churches have separated from her, she alone has never separated from any other Church on earth, and consequently, that she alone is the accredited representative of that Church founded by our Divine Redeemer, against which He has promised that " the gates of hell shall not prevail." Now, we certainly

* " A Discourse on the Religion anciently professed by the Irish and British." First printed in 1631.

know that it was the Roman Catholic Church which existed in Ireland *before the Reformation*, and from this very fact we argue that it was the same Church which existed in Ireland *from the beginning of Christianity in the country*, unless it can be proved that a *change* of religion was established *between* that early period and the time of the Reformation. It must surely be admitted, that the *presumption* is strongly in favor of the continued identity of the same form of Christianity, unless there be clear evidence to the contrary. But it is impossible to show that any such change ever took place, either in the establishment of a *new Church*, or in the introduction of *new doctrines;* and therefore, whether we regard the question as an historical fact, or as a theological principle, we must come to the conclusion, that the religion of the country *before* the Reformation, which is *still* professed by the vast majority of the people of Ireland, is essentially the *same* with the *religion of St. Patrick*, and the other founders and Saints of the Irish Church in ancient times. But if this be denied—if it be said, that the doctrines of the Church of Rome were the corruptions of a *later* age—we have, surely, a right to ask, When did these doctrines *begin* to be introduced into Ireland? and how came they to be universally received in the country? how did it happen that they were unanimously adopted by Bishops, Clergy, and Laity, without any opposition to the innovation? We all know that a change took place in the 16th Century, but where can we find a trace in history, of any change between the 5th and 16th Centuries? And, if it be said that these early corruptions were gradually introduced into the Church, we reply that this is a mere assertion, contrary to all the facts of history. We are told, indeed, of the Synod of Cashel, held in the year 1172, which is described by a learned Irish Protestant author as "the turning point and pivot of our Church history," because he says that then "our own Church, that had been originally free and independent, was, in the 12th Century, reduced into obedience and subjection to the Bishop of Rome."[*] But there is not the slightest authority for this statement in any account of the proceedings of the Synod. It was convened by order of Henry II., for the purpose of regulating certain matters of Ecclesiastical discipline, and it was presided over by Chris-

---

[*] King's Church History, Pref. p. xviii.

tian, Bishop of Lismore, as the Pope's Legate in Ireland. The most complete account of it has been given by Giraldus Cambrensis, who lived at the time, and who has transmitted to us a copy of the Canons passed on that occasion. There is no allusion whatever to the Pope's Supremacy, or to any other point of doctrine. The most important of them is the last, which provides "that all Divine matters be henceforth conducted agreeably to the practice of the holy Church, *according as observed by the Anglican Church.*"* The object of this Canon was to promote a more perfect uniformity, in the adoption of the same ritual by the two Churches of England and Ireland, which were now more closely united together in their civil policy ; but there is no trace to be found of any attempt to procure from the Irish Church a recognition of the claims of the Apostolic See, simply because these claims had never been disputed at any period of her former history. The invasion of Henry II. was the commencement of that unhappy spirit of hostility between the two countries, which has existed ever since in a greater or less degree. That spirit had its origin in the feelings of national antipathy, though it was afterwards greatly increased by religious animosities. The Synod of Cashel itself was rather of a *political* than of an *ecclesiastical* nature. It was ostensibly convened for the reformation of irregularities in the Church, but its real object was to establish the English dominion in Ireland. It is candidly admitted by the late Mr. Moore, in his History of Ireland, that "even at that period, when all were of one Faith, the Church of the government, and the Church of the people, in Ireland, were almost as much separated from each other by difference in race, language, political feeling, and even Ecclesiastical discipline, as they have been at any period since, by difference in Creeds."† It should be remembered that the circumstances of the times were peculiarly favorable to Henry's plan of annexing Ireland to his own dominions. The Pope himself was an Englishman ; and, influenced by the love of his country, and a desire to gratify the king, Adrian IV. had granted a Bull, in the year 1155, authorising Henry II. to take possession of Ireland, " for the purpose of extending the boundaries of the Church, of announcing to unlearned and rude people the truth of the Christian Faith, and extirpating the weeds of

---

* Lanigan, Vol. IV. p. 207.
  Moore's Hist. of Ireland, Vol. III. p. 119.

vices from the field of the Lord,"· -and further, with the express condition, that Henry would "preserve the rights of the Church inviolate, and that, as he promised to do, he would take care that a penny should be annually paid from every house to St. Peter and the holy Roman Church."* It does not appear, however, that this latter condition was ever complied with—there is nothing about it in the transactions of the Synod of Cashel, and when Henry had carried the Bull into effect, he seems to have forgotten entirely about the collection of the Peter pence, and indeed the failure of these conditions is expressly mentioned in the complaint of the Irish Nobles to Pope John XXII. in the 14th Century.† But, with respect to the particular Canon in question, it is very probable that various Liturgies had been used in different parts of the Irish Church before the 12th Century; and from this circumstance, it has been argued that the old Irish Church could not have been subject to Rome, as otherwise the Roman Missal would have been universally adopted in Ireland. But this is a mere cavil, as it is well known that the *variety of Liturgies* in the Church never did, and does not, at the present day, interfere with the great principle of *Catholic unity*. Especially was this the case in ancient times, when almost every national Church had its own peculiar Liturgy, and sometimes several different Liturgies in the same country, each containing some special rites and ceremonies of its own, with the full approbation of the Apostolic See. The Roman Missal, or the Liturgy of St. Peter, was, in a great measure, peculiar to the local Church of Rome, and was not required to be generally adopted in other Churches. The Salisbury Missal was the Liturgy chiefly used in England in Catholic times, though, in some Dioceses, the York, Lincoln, Hereford, and Bangor Missals were adopted before the Reformation ; but since the time of Pope Pius V. the Roman Missal is most commonly followed throughout the Catholic world. Still, however, this uniformity is not universally enjoined. Thus we find that the Greek, Syrian, Armenian, and other Liturgies are still used in the city of Rome itself. So is the Ambrosian Liturgy in Milan, and the Mozarabic Liturgy in Toledo, while several religious Orders of the Church have their own peculiar Liturgies, all

---

* O'Halloran's Hist. of Ireland, Vol. III. p. 372. (Ed. 1803.)
† King's Church Hist. p. 1123.

different from the Roman, and all in perfect harmony with it, and with each other*.

But it is said that the ancient Irish Church differed from the Roman in the time of the celebration of Easter, and this is the great argument which is continually employed to prove that the Supremacy of the Pope could not have been acknowledged in Ireland. Time will not allow me to enter into the history of this controversy, to which I adverted in my former Lecture with reference to the British Churches, which adopted the same mode of computation with the Irish. It is sufficient to remark that this was originally a mere point of discipline, though, after its final decision by the Church, it involved a higher principle, and ultimately led to the schismatical act of adherence to local customs, in opposition to the universal practice of the Church. The rule for finding Easter was settled by the great Council of Nice— the same Astronomical Cycle was also adopted in all the Churches— but an improved Cycle was *afterwards* introduced, and adopted by the Roman, while the British and Irish Churches, owing to their great distance and isolated situation, still continued to use the old and incorrect Cycle, which sometimes led to the difference of a month in the time of keeping Easter in the same year, between them and other Churches, and which for a long time they obstinately refused to exchange for the corrected system. But, though they were unwilling to depart from their ancient traditions, they never questioned the authority of the See of Rome to decide all controversies of faith, and, in fact, it was on this very ground that they finally conformed to the rule which had been adopted by all other Catholic countries. Yet some authors have represented this circumstance, not only as a proof of their opposition to Rome, but also, as a strong presumptive argument in favor of the *Eastern* origin of the Irish Church, before the mission of St. Patrick. But, in the first place, there is not the slightest historical evidence in favor of this opinion—in the second place, the Irish time of keeping Easter was undoubtedly derived from St. Patrick, who was certainly *not* a Greek or Asiatic missionary—and in the third place, the Irish time of keeping Easter was *never the same* as that of the Oriental Churches, while it was originally the same as the Roman. It is very strange that so many writers should have fallen into the mistake of supposing that the

* Lanigan, Vol. I. p. 13.

Irish agreed with the Eastern Christians on this point, when it is expressly mentioned by Bede, that they always observed Easter on the *Sunday* between the 14th and 20th days of the month[*], whereas the Easterns always observed it on the 14th day of the month, *on whatever day of the week* it might fall, and thus there is not even the shadow of foundation for this objection.

But there is another historical objection to which I must briefly refer, and the more so, because it is founded on an erroneous statement of the great historian of the Catholic Church. It has been frequently argued that, in the celebrated controversy on " the Three Chapters," in the 6th Century, the Irish Church took part with the condemned opinions, in opposition to the Church of Rome, and consequently that the Supremacy of the Pope was practically denied by this act. Now what is the foundation of this argument? It is the following remarkable passage in the " Ecclesiastical Annals" of Cardinal Baronius, in which he says—" all the Bishops that were in Ireland rose up with one accord in the most determined spirit of zeal for the defence of the Three Chapters. And they were guilty moreover of this further wickedness, that when they had perceived that the Roman Church was equally determined in condemning the Three Chapters, and strengthening the Fifth Synod by her adherence, they at once separated from her, and joined themselves with the rest of the schismatics that were in Italy, or Africa, or other places, puffed up with the vain conceit that, by defending the Acts of the Council of Chalcedon, they were making a stand in support of the Catholic faith."[†] This is strong language indeed, and from it Abp. Ussher concludes, that " the Bishops of Ireland did not take all the resolutions of the Church of Rome for undoubted oracles."[‡] But, after all, this extraordinary statement of Baronius is completely founded on a strange mistake, and there is no evidence that the Irish Church took any part whatever in that question. Baronius relies solely on the authority of Pope Gregory the Great, by whom he thinks that they were convinced of their errors, and he refers to two of Pope Gregory's Epistles for proof. In both of them, the proof entirely depends on the genuineness of one word, " Hibernia," con-

---

[*] Bedæ Hist. Eccles. Lib. II. Cap. iv. Lib. III. Cap. iii. xvii. xxv.
[†] Baronii Annal. Eccles. ad an. 566 et 604.
[‡] Ussher's Discourse, p. 86. (Ed. 1815.)

tained in the superscription of these Epistles, and it is now the general opinion of all learned men, in accordance with the critical Benedictine Edition of St. Gregory's Works, that this word has been incorrectly inserted in the text of the old editions, and that the true reading' is " Istria" in the one case, and " Iberia" in the other*. This has been clearly proved from internal as well as external evidence—indeed the account of Baronius is directly contrary to that of St. Columbanus himself, who, in a letter to Pope Boniface IV. shortly after the time of Gregory the Great, expressly affirms that Ireland was entirely free from all heresy and schism† ; and thus it appears that this whole piece of history has no real foundation in fact, and the argument founded upon it falls to the ground at once.

These, then, are the principal arguments that have been advanced to prove that the doctrines of the ancient Church of Ireland were different from those of the modern Church of Rome ; and I think it must be admitted that the attempt is a total failure, even if we had no further evidence on the subject of the particular doctrines held by the Fathers of the Irish Church. Let us, then, take a few points in positive proof of the Ecclesiastical connexion between Rome and Ireland in ancient times.

Now, in the first place, it is certain that *Palladius and St. Patrick were sent on the Irish Mission by the Pope,* and thus the first great event in its Ecclesiastical history connects Ireland with Rome, as the " Mother and mistress of all Churches." But we have still clearer proof that the primitive Irish Church acknowledged the Supremacy of the See of Rome. Among the Canons ascribed to St. Patrick, there is one, on the subject of appeals to Rome, which is expressed in these brief but decisive terms—" If any questions arise in this Island, *let them be referred to the Apostolic See.*"‡ But the meaning of this Canon is more fully expressed in another Canon, which is attributed to a Synod held by St. Patrick—the substance of which is this, that " if a difficult cause may occur, which cannot be easily decided by the Irish Prelates, and the See of Armagh, *it shall be sent to the Apostolic See, that is to the Chair of the Apostle*

---

* S. Gregorii M. Epist. Lib. II. Ep. 51, and Lib. XI. Ep. 67—Opp. Tom. II pp. 614, 1116. (Ed. Ben.)

† King's Church Hist. p. 942.

‡ S. Patricii Opuscula p. 159.

Peter, which hath the authority of the City of Rome.'' Archbishop Ussher quotes these Canons, and he seems quite puzzled by
them. He says he does not well know what credit is to be given to
them—he admits, indeed, that " it is most likely that St. Patrick had
a special regard to the Church of Rome, from whence he was sent for
the conversion of this Island,''† but then he tries to evade their force
by a mere quibble, asserting that they do not expressly affirm the infal-
libility of the Church of Rome in all future times, and that the Irish
Bishops themselves afterwards refused to submit to the Pope's decision, in the case of the " Three Chapters," according to the statement of Baronius, which has been already shown to be quite unfounded. But we have a remarkable illustration of the meaning of
these Canons, on the first serious occasion of controversy which pre-
sented itself, relative to the time of Easter, though this is the very
instance which has been so strongly quoted on the other side. In the
year 633, we find that, after a long dissension, it was resolved by the
Synod of Leighlin, that "whereas, according to a Synodical Canon,
every important Ecclesiastical inquiry should be referred to the head
of cities : some wise and humble persons should be sent to Rome, as
children to their mother." This resolution was carried into effect,
and the result was the adoption of the Roman Paschal Cycle, in the
South of Ireland, in accordance with the decision of the Pope. We
have a particular account of these proceedings recorded in the Paschal
Epistle of St. Cummian, who enters fully into the whole question
about Easter, and insists upon the necessity of submitting to the
authority of the Catholic Church, in preference to national traditions*.
He quotes, with approbation, the language of St. Jerome in his Epistle
to Pope Damasus, in which he says—" If any one is in communion
with the Chair of St. Peter, he is on my side."‡ And, after dwelling
strongly on the doctrine of St. Cyprian and other holy Fathers,
on the unity of the Church, he asks—" Can any thing more per-
nicious be conceived as to the Mother Church, than to say—Rome errs
—Jerusalem errs—Alexandria errs—Antioch errs—the whole world
errs—the Scots and Britons alone are right ?"§ Such was the argu-

---

* Lanigan, Vol. II. p. 391.
† Ussher's Discourse, p. 84.
‡ Lanigan, Vol. II. p. 396. King, Vol. I. p. 158.
§ S. Hieron. Opp. Tom. I. p. 437. (Ed. Vallars.)

ment by which St. Cummian endeavored to show the absurdity of following a *part* of the Church, in opposition to the *whole*. And I cannot help remarking here, that it is this very absurdity which has been adopted by the " Scots and Britons" of the present day, that is, by the United Church of England and Ireland, as expressed in the 19th of the 39 Articles, almost in the very words condemned by St. Cummian—"As the Churches of Jerusalem, Alexandria, and Antioch have erred, so also the Church of Rome hath erred, not only in their living and manner of ceremonies, but also in matters of faith." Such is the judgment pronounced by the *modern Church against all the ancient Churches of Christendom.*—involving questions infinitely more serious than that which formed the subject of dispute in the 7th Century.

I shall add but one testimony more on this point, that of the great St. Columbanus, in his celebrated Epistle to Pope Boniface IV. in the year 613. Among other passages, he uses the following remarkable expressions—" *We Irishmen,* dwelling at the very end of the earth, *are all disciples of SS. Peter and Paul,* and of all the disciples who wrote the divine Canon, according to the Holy Ghost, receiving nothing beyond the Evangelical and Apostolical doctrine. There has been no Jew, nor heretic, nor schismatic, among us ; but the Catholic Faith, as it was delivered at the first by you, that is, the successors of the holy Apostles, is still maintained among us with unshaken fidelity. . . . For *we,* indeed, as I have already stated, *are warmly attached to the Chair of St. Peter.* And, great as is the renown and celebrity of Rome, it is by means of *that Chair alone* that she is illustrious with us. . . . And on account of the two Apostles, Peter and Paul, you are almost celestial—*and Rome is the head of the Churches of the world.*"[*] Now, what can be more clear and decisive than this language? It is true that he adds an apparent exception in favor of Jerusalem—" saving the singular prerogative of the place of the Lord's resurrection"—but this evidently relates to the circumstance of our blessed Lord's personal connexion with that city, and not to any Primacy of spiritual jurisdiction in the Universal Church, which was never claimed for the Church of Jerusalem.

Again—with reference to the doctrine of the Blessed Eucharist and

---

[*] Lanigan, Vol. II. p. 290. King, p. 942, 952, 953.

the Sacrifice of the Mass, the constant language of the old Irish writers clearly attests the unity of faith between them and the present Church of Rome on these points. Thus we find that St. Patrick himself, as well as the later Irish Divines, frequently describe the Mass as "the *sacrifice* of salvation,"—" the mysteries of the *sacrifice*,"—" the *sacred mysteries* of the Eucharist,"—and even in the ordinary narrative of biography, the celebration of Mass is expressed as the act of "*making the body of Christ.*" Thus Adamnan, who lived in the 7th Century, mentions, in his Life of St. Columbkill, that the Saint requested a certain Bishop " to make the body of Christ, according to the usual custom." In like manner, the consecration of the Eucharist is called by those writers " the *immolation* of the holy *sacrifice* of the Lord," and the sacramental communion is expressed by the terms of " receiving the *body and blood of Christ.*" Thus Cogitosus, in his Life of St. Bridget, in describing the Church of Kildare, says, that the Bishop entered with his Clergy by one door, " to *immolate* the holy *sacrifice* of the Lord," and that the Abbess and Nuns entered by another door, " that they might enjoy the banquet of the body and blood of Jesus Christ". Another phrase for the celebration of Mass, with the old Irish Church, was the "*offering* of the body of Christ." Thus, in the first Life of St. Kieran, it is said that, on every Christmas night, after his community had received the sacrifice from his hand, he used to go to the Nunnery " to *offer* the body of Christ." Still more expressly, St. Columbanus lays it down in his rules, that confession be required diligently before Mass, lest a person receive it unworthily—" for" he says, " the altar is the tribunal of Christ, *and His body, which is there with His blood,* marks out those who approach in an unworthy state." Surely such expressions as these clearly prove that the Catholic doctrine of the real presence was the received doctrine of the ancient Irish Church.

On the doctrine of Purgatory, and Prayers for the Dead, the evidence is equally conclusive. Indeed, Abp. Ussher fully admits the practice of offering up the Eucharistic Sacrifice for the dead in Christ, though he maintains that it was *only* intended as a sacrifice of *thanksgiving* for their salvation, and not of *propitiation* for the remission of the temporal penalty of their sins*. He refers to several instances of this nature, and among them, to that of St Columbkill, on the occasion of

---

* Ussher's Religion of the Irish, p. 27.

the death of St. Brendan. " I must to-day," says the Saint, " although I be unworthy, celebrate the holy mysteries of the Eucharist,
on account of my veneration for that soul which, this night, carried
beyond the starry firmament between the holy Choirs of Angels, as-
cended into paradise." Another case mentioned by him is that of
Magnus, who said to Bishop Tozzo, who came to visit him on his
death-bed—" I believe in the mercy of God, that my soul shall rejoice
in the freedom of immortality. Yet I beseech thee, that thou wilt not
cease to help me a sinner, and my soul, with thy holy prayers." Immediately after his death, the Bishop said to Theodorus—" Let us go
to the Church, and be careful to offer healthful sacrifices to the Lord
for so dear a friend." This case, however, evidently proves nothing
in favor of Ussher's view ; and, in fact, his opinion is a mere *theory*
invented to meet a difficulty, and to account for a fact which cannot
be denied. It is certain, indeed, that there was such a distinction as
that to which he referred ; but while he held that all these sacrifices
were *only thanksgivings*, we find that this explanation is directly over-
turned by an old Canon of the Irish Church (which is expressed almost in the words of St. Augustine*) in which it is declared that the
Church offers to God for the departed souls in four ways—one of
which is, that " for the *very good*, the oblations are mere *thanksgivings*"; and another is, that " for those *not very good*, they are made for
the *obtaining of full remission*." But Ussher takes *one* class of examples,
while he entirely *omits another*—though it is certain that the ancient
Irish Christians constantly adopted this practice ; and in an old Irish
MS. Missal of the 7th Century, discovered by Mabillon, there are two
forms of prayer for the Dead, one in general, and the other for a departed
Priest.† And yet, some persons have brought an objection from one of
the Canons of St. Patrick's Synod, which is entitled—" Of the Obla-
tion for the Dead," and is thus expressed—" Hear the Apostle saying,
There is a sin unto death, I do not say that for it any one pray. And
the Lord—Do not give the Holy to dogs. For he who will not deserve
to receive the Sacrifice during his life, *how can it help him after his
death*?"‡ It has been thought that this Canon condemns altogether

---

* S. August, Opp. Tom. VI. p. 233.

† Lanigan, Vol. IV. p. 372.

‡ S. Patricii Opuscula, p. 105.

the practice of offering for the dead, but it is clear that the inference to be drawn from it is just the reverse, on the principle that *the exception proves the rule.* It certainly prohibits the act of offering for those who died in *mortal sin*, and were unworthy to receive " the sacrifice" *during their lives*; but surely this very prohibition implies that *all others* are proper subjects for the oblations and sacrifices of the Church. It is the doctrine of the Church, that there is no redemption from hell, and therefore she never prays for the souls in perdition. To *this case alone* the Canon applies; and therefore it teaches that the ordinary rule of oblations for the dead, includes all her departed members, who were supposed, while alive, to be worthy of being admitted to the holy communion. But another objection has been derived from a passage in the Treatise " on the Three Habitations," which are described as Heaven, Earth, and Hell, without any mention of Purgatory*. It has been frequently argued from this passage, that St. Patrick did not hold the doctrine of Purgatory, or he would not have omitted it here. But, in the first place, as remarked before, it is now generally agreed, that this is not a genuine Work of St. Patrick. But further, there is nothing in it contrary to the Catholic doctrine, as the writer is not referring to any *temporary* place of purification in the intermediate state, which is only visited by a certain *part* of the human race, but to the *permanent* habitation of the good and bad, to which they will be finally consigned in the other world; nor does he say that *all* the just are admitted to heaven *immediately* after death, which is the great question in dispute; so that this Tract, whoever might have written it really affords no argument on either side.

As to the Invocation of Saints, we have already observed an instance of it incidentally mentioned by St. Patrick, as practised by himself; and it is a singular fact, that Ussher himself, while trying to prove that the ancient Irish Church held Protestant doctrines, entirely omits all allusions to this subject, thus tacitly admitting the general prevalence of the practice. We find that an ancient Life of St. Bridget, written in the 7th Century, in Irish verse, often invokes her in the course of it, and concludes with these words—" there are two holy Virgins in Heaven, who may undertake my protection, *Mary, and Bridget, on whose patronage let us depend.*" Again, we find that Dungal, a most learned Irishman, formally defended this and other Catholic doctrines,

---

* S. Patricii Opuscula, p. 280.

in opposition to Claudius. Indeed, it is remarked by the modern Protestant historian of the Irish Church—" it appears plainly that, by the close of the 8th Century, the grossest corruption, in this particular, had become prevalent."[*] The same author remarks also, that " the language used in Divine Service in these countries in the earliest ages, appears to have been always the Latin, as far as we can learn from any evidence that remains of ancient documents relating to the subject."[†]

But it is quite unnecessary to enter into further proofs, in order to show that the whole system of Christian doctrine, held by the ancient Irish Church, was essentially the same with that held by all the other branches of the Universal Church in those times, as well as by the Roman Catholic Church in the present day. It would be easy to show, indeed, that the Irish Church, as well as other national churches, had its own peculiarities as to *local customs*, which are merely matters of *discipline*, and do not affect any article of the Christian *Faith* or doctrine. It will be remembered that I am speaking of the earliest period in the Church History of Ireland, long before the commencement of any connexion with England, and consequently we have here a complete refutation of the assertion, that the Papal Supremacy, and other doctrines, were first introduced into Ireland in the 12th Century. I have endeavored to investigate this subject in a historical point of view, and to state the facts of the case, which are equally open to the impartial inquiry of Protestants and Catholics. My object is the pursuit of truth, without reference to preconceived opinions of any kind. But the facts of Church History have a very important connexion with the discovery of religious truth. Human opinions are constantly changing, but authentic facts remain always the same. Now Christianity itself is a *fact*, and not a mere *opinion*—it is not an idea communicated to each individual mind, but it is a divine revelation made to the world 1800 years ago, and transmitted by the Church to each successive generation. And therefore, while we are attempting to ascertain, by historical evidence, what was the religious system delivered to the Irish Church by St. Patrick, in the 5th Century, we are really going back to the fountain

---

[*] King, Vol. I. p. 368.
[†] Ibid. p. 369.

head of all true religion—the teaching of our Blessed Lord and His inspired Apostles; and we are joining together the several links in the chain which connect this present hour with the day of Pentecost, when the Church of Christ was founded on earth by the descent of the Holy Ghost from Heaven. And if it be maintained that the Roman Catholic Church in Ireland is corrupt in doctrine *at this day*, then it must have been equally corrupt *in the time of St. Patrick;* and if the religion which *he* taught was corrupt, then it must have been corrupt *from the beginning*, for all the links in the chain are inseparably connected together, and the whole deposit of the Faith is thus identified with the Divine Tradition flowing from the very Throne of God, descending into the bosom of the Church, and preserved through an unbroken succession of Bishops, Pastors, Doctors, Saints, and Martyrs, united in communion with the Chair of St. Peter, and the "One, Holy, Catholic, and Apostolic Church" of Christ on earth.

There is much truth, indeed, in the remarks of the learned Protestant, Dr. Phelan, with reference to the hereditary feelings of our countrymen, as expressed in the following language—" The Irish are a fondly national people; they know little of their ancestors, but they believe of them every thing which enters into their conceptions of worth and greatness, and they feel a high, although mournful consolation in turning from their own condition to the supposed freedom and glory and happiness of other times. These principles have been incorporated into their Creed, they receive their religion as the last bequest, and the last token of their almost canonised forefathers, and they cling to it with a devoted and desperate fidelity. Their religion is made to look venerable through the vista of antiquity—interesting in the garb and attitude of decay; and this interest assumes a dearer, and this veneration a holier character, from the sympathy of the Church with the fallen fortunes of her children. Thus the faith of a zealous Roman Catholic, though not that which either the truly spiritual or the truly philosophic would prefer, comes upon him with the romantic power of a picturesque and melancholy grandeur. Its influence is aided by the habits of a rural life—it is recalled by the ruined Abbey, and the tottering Round Tower—it is studiously associated with the hearths, the tombs, and the altars of its progenitors. It is similarly connected with all those of whatsoever country, who in the first and purest ages of the Gospel, departed this life in the faith and fear of God, until through a long line of Martyrs and Confessors—through St. Patrick—through the Apostles—it finally blends itself with the Saviour of the world."

Yes, my Catholic Brethren! you have just reason—I will not say, to be proud of such an honor, but rather, to be deeply thankful to God, for His distinguishing grace in making you heirs, without any merits on your part, of that holy faith which you have inherited from your ancestors, and through them, from the glorious Saints and Founders of the Irish Church in ancient times. But, at the same time, let us remember that the Catholic religion is not confined to one country or one nation. No! it is, as its name implies, universal—it includes every nation under heaven; and all earthly and national distinctions must be comparatively forgotten, and absorbed in this spiritual relation that exists among the members of " the Church of the Living God." We must be careful to show by the example of a holy life, that Catholics do not belong to any mere Irish party, associated together for political or ecclesiastical purposes, and separated from those of every other race by their Celtic origin and habits. In this view, a true Catholic Christian is not an Irishman—nor an Englishman—nor a Frenchman—nor an American, however attached he may be to the land of his birth, or adoption. He belongs to no country in this world. He is a stranger and a pilgrim on earth—he is a member of the Family of God, and a citizen of the heavenly Jerusalem—he is " not of the world, as Christ was not of the world." But while every country has its own representatives in the Church of God, each of them still retains some marks of its national peculiarities; and while we cherish, with affectionate veneration, the memory of those blessed and holy men and women, who have shed so bright a lustre over the annals of our country by their zealous and devoted lives of piety and virtue, let us hope and pray that the spirit of faith and love that animated their hearts may be revived among the children of the Church to the latest generations ; and that the fair land of Erin may again be justly distinguished by that sacred name by which she was recognised in the days of old, and may shine forth in the beauties of holiness, conspicuous among all the other nations of the Christian world, in the true character of her own glorious and immortal title—as the " ISLAND OF SAINTS."